S0-AVW-718

THE AMAZING ADVENTURES OF THE DC SUPER-PETS!™

Trouble on Paradise Island

by Steve Korté
illustrated by Art Baltazar

Wonder Woman created by
William Moulton Marston

PICTURE WINDOW BOOKS
a capstone imprint

Published by Picture Window Books, an imprint of Capstone.
1710 Roe Crest Drive
North Mankato, Minnesota 56003
www.capstonepub.com

Cataloging-in-Publication Data is available at the Library of Congress website.
ISBN: 978-1-5158-7179-8 (library binding)
ISBN: 978-1-5158-7324-2 (paperback)
ISBN: 978-1-5158-7187-3 (eBook PDF)

Summary: An enemy has appeared at Paradise Island! Will Wonder Woman and her superpowered Kanga, Jumpa, be able to protect their hidden home?

Designed by Ted Williams
Design Elements by Shutterstock/SilverCircle

Printed and bound in the United States of America.
PA117

TABLE OF CONTENTS

She is a high-jumping animal
known as a Kanga.
She has a superpowered tail
and can run extra-fast.
She is Wonder Woman's
loyal friend.
These are . . .

THE AMAZING ADVENTURES OF

Jumpa the Kanga!

Super-Pets on Paradise Island

There is a secret island hidden from the rest of the world. It is called

Paradise Island.

Wonder Woman was born there. When she was a little girl, she had a special pet. That pet was a Kanga named Jumpa.

Kangas are like kangaroos, but they can jump farther and run faster. Kangas are only found on Paradise Island. Every creature that lives there is gifted with power, strength, and beauty.

CHAPTER 2 DANGER!

An evil witch named Circe has been spotted nearby!

Wonder Woman finds Jumpa in the stable. “We need to find Circe!” says Wonder Woman.

There are other animals in the stable. One is a tiny Kanga mouse named Leepa.

Leepa pokes her head out of a pile of straw.

"I want to go too!" says Leepa.

"Leepa, you are too small. You should stay behind," Jumpa says.

Wonder Woman and Jumpa rush out of the stable and head to the beach.

When no one is looking, Leepa runs after them.

Wonder Woman and her Kanga find Circe standing on the shore.

A dangerous Harpy is flying above Circe's head. A Harpy is a horrible creature. It is half-human, half-vulture.

Wonder Woman gets ready to throw her tiara at the Harpy.

But the Harpy grabs the tiara with her claws!

Jumpa acts quickly. She throws her own tiara.

Jumpa's tiara knocks the Harpy out cold.

The creature tumbles through the air. It drops Wonder Woman's tiara.

Jumpa hops up and catches the falling tiara. She hands it to Wonder Woman.

"Thanks, Jumpa!" says Wonder Woman. "That was quick thinking!"

CHAPTER 3

Kanga Kicks Save the Day

Circe starts chanting the words to a magical spell.

Wonder Woman spins her magic lasso. Then she throws it at the witch.

The lasso wraps around Circe, but it's too late. The witch's spell has caused a giant wave to form in the ocean.

Paradise Island is going to flood when the wave hits the shore!

Just then, Leepa the Kanga mouse runs onto the beach.

Jumpa has an idea.

Both Super-Pets use their lightning-fast feet to dig a hole.

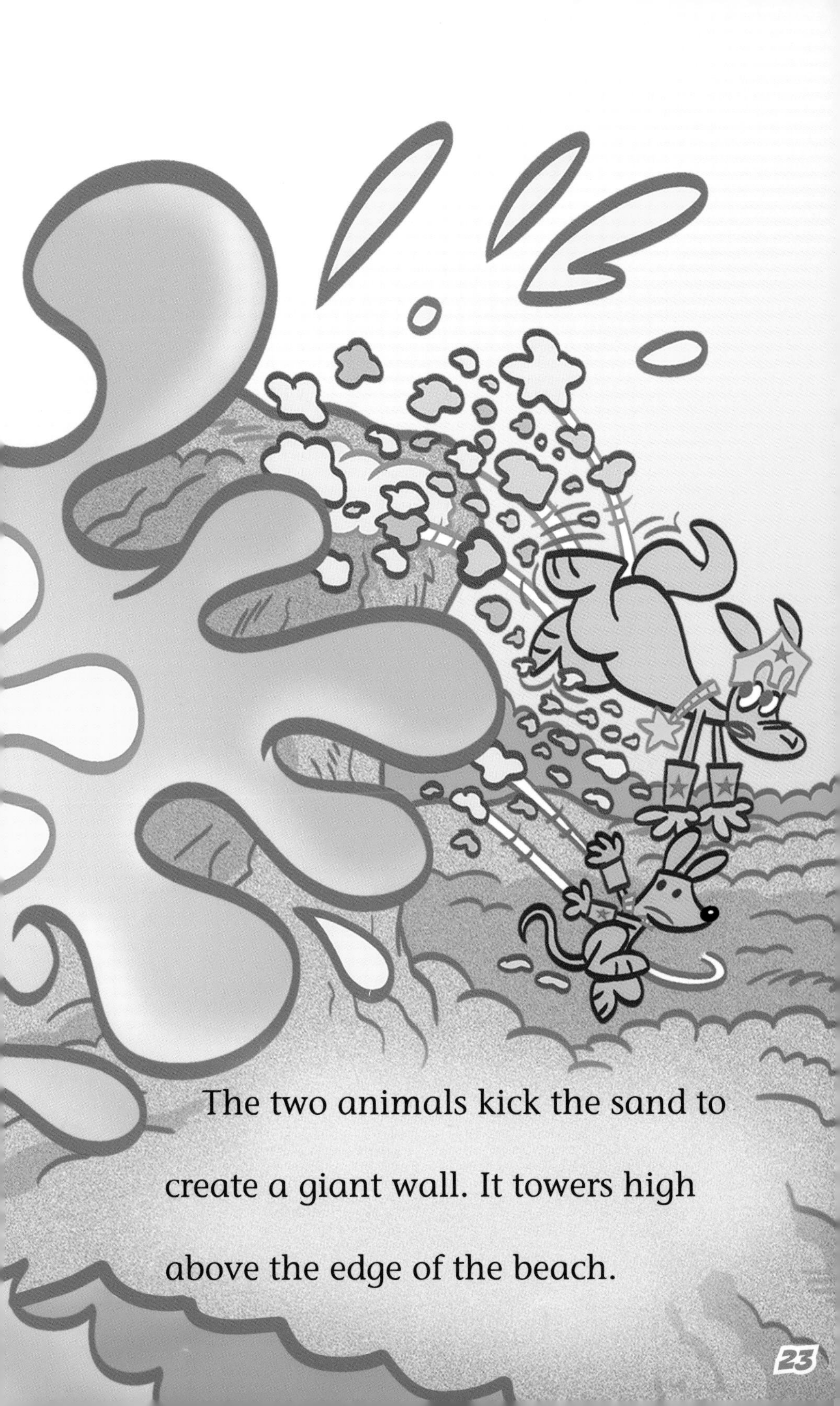

The two animals kick the sand to create a giant wall. It towers high above the edge of the beach.

The huge wave slams into the sandy mountain. The sand stops the water. Paradise Island is saved!

Wonder Woman is going to take Circe and the Harpy far away from Paradise Island.

But first she reaches over to hug Jumpa and Leepa.

"Your smart thinking and teamwork saved the day!" says Wonder Woman. "I know I can always count on my high-jumping friends!"

AUTHOR!

Steve Korté is the author of many books for children and young adults. He worked at DC Comics for many years, editing more than 600 books about Superman, Batman, Wonder Woman, and the other heroes and villains in the DC Universe. He lives in New York City with his husband, Bill, and their super-cat, Duke.

ILLUSTRATOR!

Famous cartoonist Art Baltazar is the creative force behind *The New York Times* bestselling, Eisner Award-winning DC Comics' Tiny Titans; co-writer for Billy Batson and the Magic of Shazam, Young Justice, Green Lantern Animated (Comic); and artist/co-writer for the awesome Tiny Titans/Little Archie crossover, Superman Family Adventures, Super Powers, and Itty Bitty Hellboy! Art is one of the founders of Aw Yeah Comics comic shop and the ongoing comic series! Aw yeah, living the dream! He stays home and draws comics and never has to leave the house! He lives with his lovely wife, Rose, sons Sonny and Gordon, and daughter, Audrey! AW YEAH MAN! Visit him at www.artbaltazar.com

"Word Power"

chant (CHANT)—to say or sing a phrase over and over

kangaroo (kang-guh-ROO)—an Australian animal that hops on its strong rear legs

lasso (LAS-oh)—a rope formed into a loop

paradise (PAR-uh-dice)—a very beautiful place

shore (SHOR)—the place where water meets land

stable (STAY-buhl)—a building for animals

tiara (tee-AR-uh)—a piece of jewelry that looks like a small crown

unconscious (un-KON-shus)—not awake

vulture (VUHL-cher)—a large bird that eats dead animals

WRITING PROMPTS

1. Write a story with Circe as the main character. Don't forget to add the Harpy!

2. Do you have a pet? What if it had superpowers? Write a story with you as the hero and your pet as a sidekick!

3. Make a list of ways Kangas and Kanga mice are similar. Make another list of ways they are different.

DISCUSSION QUESTIONS

1. Why do you think Jumpa told Leepa to stay put?

2. Look at the illustrations of Kangas. Think about ways they could use their extra strength and power.

3. Why do you think Circe attacked Paradise Island? Think of possible reasons. Then compare your list with someone else. Did you think of the same things?

THE AMAZING ADVENTURES OF THE

Collect them all!